WITHDRAWN

D0186731

LEABHARLANN CHO. CHILL CHAINNAIGH
Kilkenny County Library
CHILDREN'S DEPARTMENT

Acc. No. KK127192

turn	Date of Return

KILKENNY COUNTY LIBRARY

KK127192

To tortoises everywhere

A Templar Book

This edition published in the UK in 2000 by Templar Publishing,
an imprint of The Templar Company plc,
Pippbrook Mill, London Road, Dorking, Surrey, RH4 1JE, UK
www.templarco.co.uk

Distributed in the UK by Ragged Bears Ltd.,
Ragged Appleshaw, Andover, Hampshire, SP11 9HX

Copyright © 1998 by The Templar Company plc

First published in the UK in 1998
Reprinted in hardback in 1999
First softback edition

All rights reserved

ISBN Hardback: 1-84011-085-6/Softback: 1-84011-014-7

Additional design by Mike Jolley
Edited by AJ Wood

This book was drawn in ink and painted in watercolour and gouache on watercolour paper.
It was set in 25pt Bernhard Modern.

Printed in Belgium

KILKENNY COUNTY
LIBRARY £4.99
Imp
Acc. No. KK124192
Class No. JE
Inv. No. 15949
10 . 7 . 00

KILKENNY COUNTY LIBRARY

THE
HARE *and* *the* TORTOISES

Retold &
Illustrated by

HELEN WARD

TEMPLAR
PUBLISHING

There once was a very fast hare…

and a very slow tortoise.

The hare hurtled everywhere causing havoc.

KILKENNY
COUNTY
LIBRARY

The tortoise

was an altogether more

thoughtful animal.

One day the hare was carelessly sprinting along
when he tripped over the tortoise and
tumbled into a spiny bush...

which hurt.

KILKENNY COUNTY LIBRARY

The hare shouted at the tortoise.

The noise attracted a crowd.

The hare called the tortoise slow-witted and stupid.

The tortoise did not say what he

thought of the hare.

Instead, he challenged the hare to a race.

The hare laughed so much that he hurt even more.

KK127192

ALBANY
COUNTY
LIBRARY

News of the challenge spread far and wide.

From all corners of the Earth an audience began to gather.

A course was marked out...

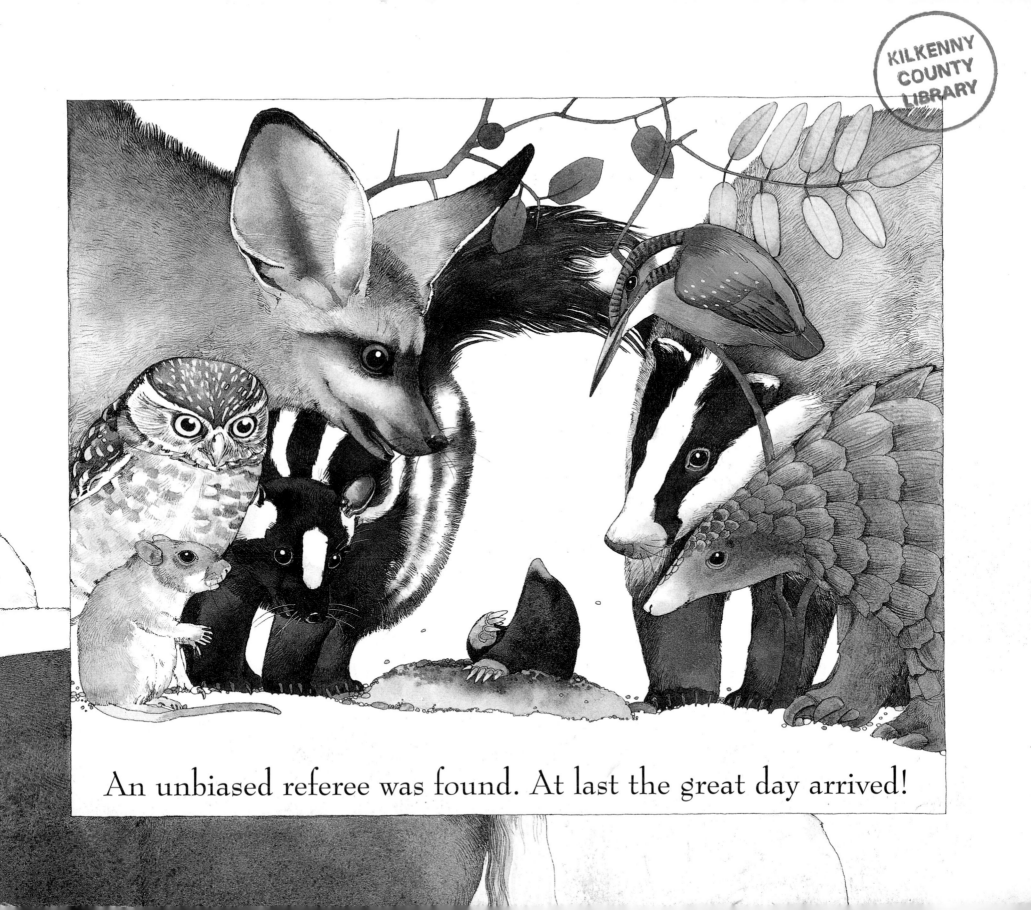

KILKENNY COUNTY LIBRARY

An unbiased referee was found. At last the great day arrived!

The referee said,

"On your marks... get set... GO!"

The hare hurtled forward

in a leap and a bound,

and was gone.

The tortoise plodded along,
slowly and steadily, one foot after the other.

He was soon left far behind.

The hare raced to
the river and
leaped...

from stone...

to stone...

towards the far bank...

...but he did not quite get to where he thought he was going.

The tortoise crossed more easily.

Next, the hare found himself in the thick of a very peculiar forest.

He was scratched and tired when he reached the other side.

KILKENNY COUNTY LIBRARY

So the hare decided to take a nap...

After all, it was obviously going to take the tortoise
a very long time indeed to scramble through
those trees…

The hare woke to find that food had grown while he slept. KILKENNY COUNTY LIBRARY
He looked around and was pleased to see that the
tortoise was so far behind he was out of sight.
So the hare had plenty of time for a long lunch.

Or so he thought...

The hare had very nearly eaten everything when he was surprised to hear the sound of cheering.

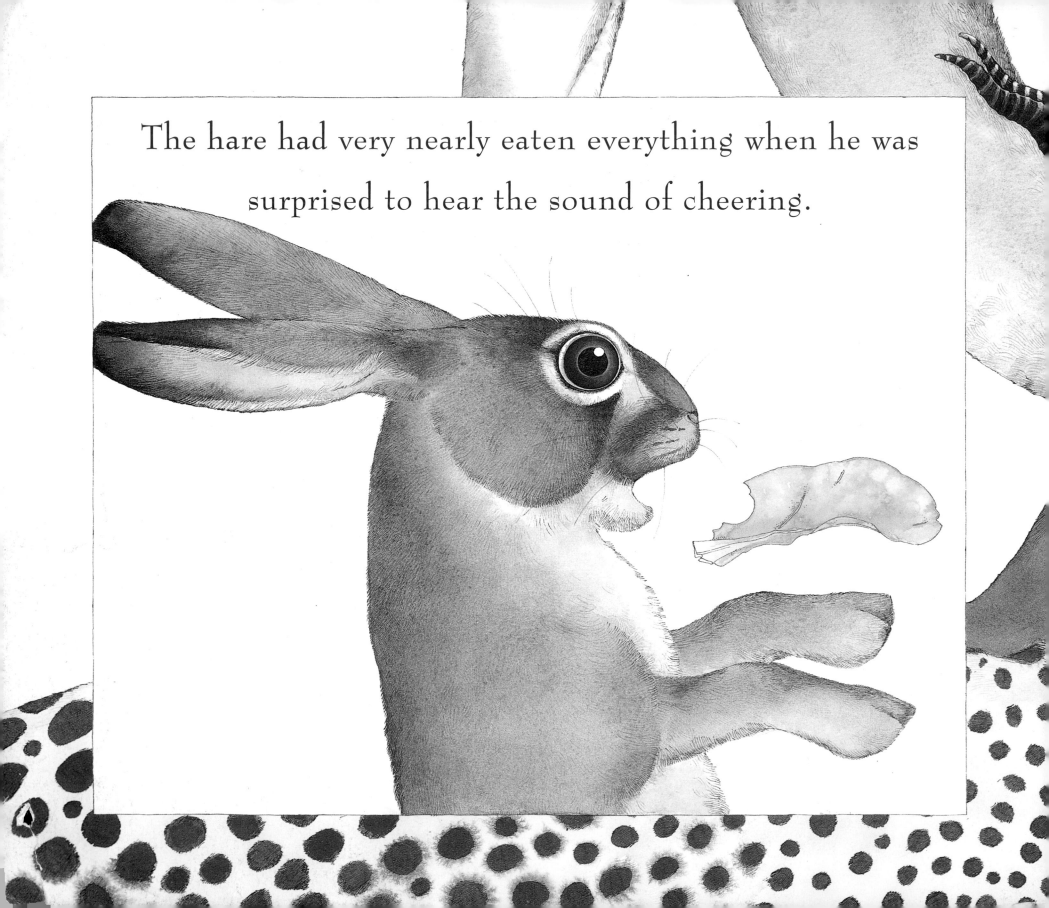

Horrified to see that the cheering was not for him,
he ran as fast as a hare with a long lunch
inside him could run.

Not fast enough! The patient, plodding tortoise

had beaten him to the finishing post.

But although the hare was not fast enough

to win the race,

he was running too fast to stop.

He fell into an even spinier bush than before...

KILKENNY
COUNTY
LIBRARY

But this time

he said nothing.

COUNTY LIBRARY

KEY TO THE
ANIMALS

There Was Once a Very Fast Hare...

All species of hare are fast runners, thanks to their long hind legs and strong leg muscles. The common brown hare *(Lepus capensis)*, illustrated throughout this book, is found in many parts of the world. It was introduced into the Americas, Australia and New Zealand from its original home in Europe so that it could be hunted for food and sport. Unlike many other small mammals, it does not burrow, but relies on its speed and vigilance to escape danger. Just as well, then, that grown male hares can reach speeds of up to 70kms per hour - faster than the world's fastest racehorse!

...And a Very Slow Tortoise

Although not the slowest creatures on the planet, tortoises have a long-standing reputation for slowness. Most move at speeds of around only 360m per hour - in other words, it would take 3 hours for our hero to travel a mere 1km! The belief that tortoises hardly move at all is not helped by the fact that, when threatened, they will not try to flee like most other animals. Instead, a frightened tortoise will stay perfectly still, retracting its head and feet beneath its armoured shell, in the hope that this will provide sufficient protection from its enemies. The tortoise painted throughout this book is known as Hermann's tortoise *(Testudo hermanni)*, the species most commonly supplied to the pet trade.

Causing Havoc

None of these creatures is speedy enough to get out of the way of a hurrying hare. In the case of the edible snail, that's hardly surprising since it is one of the slowest creatures on the planet, taking an hour to move only 4.5m. From left to right you can see an ocellated lizard, cockchafer, garden dormouse and quail, as well as the Roman or edible snail.

An Altogether More Thoughtful Animal

How thoughtful of the tortoise to provide this dwarf mongoose with a look-out post! The mongoose is a speedy snake-catcher, often kept as a pet in its original home of Asia.

The Noise Attracted A Crowd

Apart from the hare and the tortoise, the gathering crowd shows, from left to right, the dwarf mongoose, common chameleon, European quail, fennec fox, impala, short-horned grasshopper and a banded snail.

From All Corners of the Earth... (far left)

Amongst the animals that have gathered from far and wide you can see the world's fastest flying bird, the peregrine falcon. This impressive bird of prey will dive through the sky at speeds reaching 131kms per hour or more, knocking its prey of other smaller birds to the

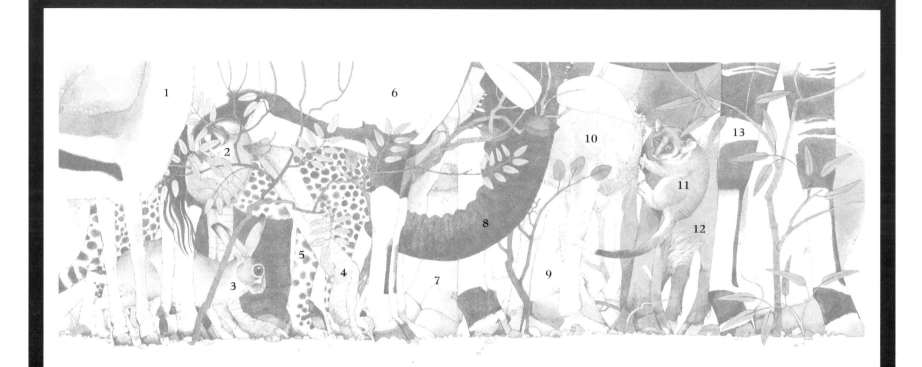

ground with a single blow of its sharp talons! At the opposite end of the scale, you can also see the dusky swallowtail butterfly, possessor of the slowest wingbeat in the insect world at 300 beats per minute!

1. Rainbow lorikeet
2. Peregrine falcon
3. Giant anteater
4. African warthog
5. White-tailed gnu
6. Dusky swallowtail butterfly
7. Polar bear
8. American bighorn sheep
9. Bat-eared fox
10. Burrowing owl
11. African gerbil
12. Spotted skunk
13. European mole
14. Kingfisher
15. Eurasian badger
16. Pangolin

But He Did Not Quite Get To Where He Thought He Was Going (previous page, right)
Like the tortoise, the hippopotamus has a reputation for being slow and lazy. True, hippos do spend practically all day resting but they can actually move quite quickly when they want to, especially when running along the river bottom. However, they are most often found standing up to their necks in river water or reed beds where they can sleep unobserved, with only their eyes and nostrils poking up above the surface.

The group of waterside dwellers also includes:

1. Pygmy goose
2. Serval
3. Green heron
4. Egyptain mongoose
5. Water chevrotain
6. White-collared kingfisher
7. Hippopotamus
8. Hare

A Very Peculiar Forest (above)
Amongst this fine array of legs are those belonging to some of the speediest creatures on earth.

The cheetah is the fastest mammal on land and can reach speeds of over 100kms per hour when chasing its prey across the African plains. It shares its home with the world's fastest land bird - the ostrich. With its powerful legs, flexible knees and two-toed feet, the ostrich is capable of reaching 72kms per hour - fast enough to outrun most of its enemies, which is just as well since it is too big to fly! Most of the other animals shown are also quick on their feet apart, of course, from the slow loris who, as its name implies, spends most of its life climbing slowly through the branches of its forest home.

1. Thomson's gazelle
2. Slow loris
3. Hare
4. Ostrich
5. Cheetah
6. Oryx
7. Indian rhinoceros
8. African elephant
9. Giraffe
10. Vicuna
11. Common ringtail
12. Red river hog
13. Okapi

When He Reached The Other Side (above)

Continuing through the forest of legs you can see:

1. Pronghorn antelope   2. Giant elephant shrew
3. Bongo   4. Giraffe
5. Gouldian finch   6. De Brazza's monkey
7. Zebra   8. Emu
9. And, of course, a very tired hare!

Plenty Of Time For A Long Lunch…

Did you spot the chinchilla (top) and northern grasshopper mouse (bottom) hiding amongst the vegetables? Both are used to living in the most inhospitable climates - the grasshopper mouse in the hot, dry deserts of North America, the chinchilla in the cold, rocky mountains of Bolivia and Chile.

The Sound Of Cheering (right)

And so we reach the end of the race! You might have expected the cheetah to have got there before the hare - after all, he is the fastest creature on earth, but somehow even the world's slowest animals have managed to make it to the finishing post as well! The three-toed sloth holds the record for being the slowest mammal, crawling along on the ground at a mere 158m per hour.

It would take the sloth over 6 hours to travel 1km. In fact, this animal spends so much time staying still that microscopic algae actually grow on its fur. However, even the sloth is faster than the red slug who would take over 3 weeks to travel that same kilometre!

1. Roadrunner - takes third place as the fastest land bird after the ostrich and emu, running at 42kms per hour.
2. Armadillo - although capable of moving quite quickly, the nine-banded armadillo holds the record for being one of sleepiest animals on earth, spending 80% of its life fast asleep, not moving at all!
3. Cheetah - the fastest land mammal at 115 kms per hour.
4. Tern - holds the record for the longest flight of any bird at 26,000kms.
5. Blackbuck - third fastest land mammal after the cheetah and pronghorn antelope, running at 80kms per hour.
6. Camel - at 16kms per hour, the camel is one of the fastest large animals in the desert.

7. Long-tailed hummingbird - hummingbirds have the fastest wingbeats in the bird world, reaching 90 beats a second in some species.
8. European mole - a champion digger, the mole can dig over 20m in a single day.
9. Giraffe - possessor of the longest legs in the animal kingdom, the giraffe can run at 50kms per hour.
10. Monarch butterfly - makes the longest journey of any insect at 3,432kms.
11. Kangaroo - this marsupial can jump almost 4m in a single giant jump and reach a speed of 45kms per hour.
12. Banded snail - Although faster than the edible snail, the banded variety would still take over a week to travel a single kilometre!
13. Three-toed sloth - the world's slowest mammal, moving at only 158m per hour.
14. Gentoo penguin - the fastest swimmer in the bird world, with a top speed of 27kms per hour.
15. Red slug - the world's slowest creature at 1.8m per hour.
16. And, to finish, who else but the slow and steady Hermann's tortoise!